USING THIS BOOK

Children learn to read by **reading**, *but they need help to begin with.*

When you have read the story on the left-hand pages aloud to the child, go back to the beginning of the book and look at the pictures together.

Encourage children to read the sentences under the pictures. If they don't know a word, give them a chance to 'guess' what it is from the illustrations, before telling them.

There are more suggestions for helping children to learn to read in the *Parent/Teacher* booklet.

British Library Cataloguing in Publication Data

McCullagh, Sheila K.
    The Gruffle. —(Puddle Lane reading programme.
    Stage 2, v. 5)
    I. Title   II. Rowe, Gavin   III. Series
    823'.914[J]   PZ7
    ISBN 0-7214-0928-8

First edition

Published by Ladybird Books Ltd Loughborough Leicestershire UK
Ladybird Books Inc Lewiston Maine 04240 USA

The Gruffle

written by SHEILA McCULLAGH
illustrated by GAVIN ROWE

Don't come in

This book belongs to:

Ladybird Books

One day, Hari and Davy went
up Puddle Lane.
They went to play in the garden
of the old house at the end of the lane.

Don't
come in

Hari and Davy
went up Puddle Lane.
They went to play in
the garden of the old house.

When they got to the garden
of the old house, they saw
a big notice hanging on the gate.
The notice said: Don't come in.

Davy and Hari saw
a notice on the gate.

"I wonder who put that notice there?"
said Hari.

"I did," said a whiffly-griffly voice
over their heads.

They looked up, and saw the Griffle
looking over the wall.

"I put the notice on the gate,"
said the Griffle.

Don't come in

The Griffle looked over
the wall. "I put the notice
on the gate," he said.

"Why can't we go into the garden?"
asked Davy.

"You mustn't go in just now,"
said the Griffle.
"The Gruffle is coming."

"Who is the Gruffle?" asked Davy.

"The Gruffle is a vanishing monster,
like me," said the Griffle.
"But he's **very** gruff and grumpy,
and he doesn't like people.
If he sees you in the garden,
he'll chase you out again."

"The Gruffle is coming,"
said the Griffle.
"The Gruffle is
a vanishing monster."

"Is he coming to live in the garden?"
asked Hari.

"No, no," said the Griffle.
"He just visits the garden
now and then.
You will know him if you see him,
because he has red ears,
and a red tail.
One of his grandfathers
was a dragon.
When the Gruffle is angry,
he puffs fire and smoke
out of his mouth."

"I think we had better go home,"
said Hari.

"Yes," said the Griffle. "Go home now.
You can come back later."

The Griffle said, "Go home now.
You can come back later."

Davy and Hari went back down
the lane. As they got to Davy's house,
they saw Peter Puffle coming
up the lane.
Peter didn't live in Puddle Lane,
but he sometimes came to stay
with Mr Puffle.
(Mr Puffle was Peter's uncle.)

Davy and Hari
saw Peter Puffle
coming up the lane.

"Hello," said Peter. "Come and play
in the garden of the old house."

"We can't play there just now,"
said Davy.
"There's a notice on the gate.
It says: Don't come in."

"Why can't we go in?" asked Peter.
"We always play there.
Nobody has ever told us not to before."

"We can't go in, because
the Gruffle is coming," said Hari.
"The Gruffle is a monster.
He's very grumpy, and
he'll chase us out of the garden."

"Come and play
in the garden,"
said Peter Puffle.

"We can't play there,"
said Davy.

"The Gruffle is coming,"
said Hari.
"The Gruffle is a monster."

"I would like to see a Gruffle,"
said Peter Puffle.
"I'm going along to the garden gate,
to have a look."

"You may not see him, but he may
still be there," said Davy.
"He's a vanishing monster.
He can disappear, whenever he wants to.
And he's very gruff and grumpy.
He'll chase you out of the garden."

"I'm going to see," said Peter.
He went on up the lane,
towards the old house.
Hari and Davy went with him.

"I would like
to see the Gruffle,"
said Peter Puffle.
He went up the lane,
to the old house.
Hari and Davy went with him.

Peter came to the gate.
He looked into the garden.
"I can't see the Gruffle," he said.

"You might only see two red ears,
or a red tail," said Davy.

"Or you might see a puff of smoke.
But the Gruffle must be there,
by this time. You mustn't go in."

Peter came to the gate.
He looked into the garden.
"I can't see the Gruffle,"
he said.

"There's no one in the garden,"
said Peter. "I'm going in."
And he opened the gate,
and went into the garden.
Davy saw two red ears over the top
of a bush.
"Come back!" he cried.
"Come back, Peter!
The Gruffle is there.
I can see two red ears."

"I won't come back," said Peter.
"There's nobody here."

Peter went into the garden.
Davy saw two red ears.
"Come back!" he cried.
"Come back, Peter.
I can see two red ears."

"I won't come back,"
said Peter.

Hari saw a long red tail.

"Come back!" he cried.

"Come back, Peter!

The Gruffle is there.

I can see a long red tail."

"I won't come back," said Peter.

"There's nobody here."

Hari saw a red tail.
"Come back!" he cried.
"Come back, Peter.
I can see a red tail."

"I won't come back,"
said Peter.

Davy saw a puff of smoke coming
from behind the old tree.
"Come back!" he cried.
"Come back, Peter!
I can see a puff of smoke.
When the Gruffle puffs smoke
out of his mouth,
he's feeling very angry."

"I won't come back," said Peter.
"There's nobody there.
It's just a bonfire."

Davy saw a puff of smoke.
"Come back!" he cried.
"Come back, Peter.
I can see a puff of smoke."

"I won't come back,"
said Peter.

Peter Puffle went around the tree —
and there was the Gruffle.
The Gruffle was feeling very grumpy,
and he was feeling very cross.
He wanted the garden all to himself,
and here was a boy
in the middle of it!
"What are you doing in my garden?"
roared the Gruffle. "Who are you?
And what are you doing here?"
And a big puff of smoke
came out of his mouth.

Peter Puffle saw the Gruffle.

Peter didn't stop to answer.
He fled. He ran to the gate,
and out of the garden.
He ran past Hari and Davy.
He ran down the lane,
as fast as he could.

Peter ran to the gate.
He ran out of the garden.
He ran down the lane,
as fast as he could.

Hari and Davy were just going
to run away too,
when the Gruffle saw a little mouse,
sitting on a stone.
The Gruffle gave another great roar.
There was a puff of smoke –
and the Gruffle had gone!

There was a puff of smoke —
and the Gruffle had gone!

"The Gruffle must be frightened of mice,"
said Hari.
He shut the gate,
(Peter had left it open),
and looked into the garden.
There was no sign of the Gruffle.
He had vanished.
"Let's come back after tea, and
see if the Gruffle is still there,"
said Davy.
Hari and Davy went home.

Hari shut the gate.
The Gruffle had gone.
Davy and Hari went home.

When they went back to
the end of the lane after tea,
they saw a new notice on the gate.
The notice said: Come in.

"Do you think it's safe to go in
now?" asked Hari.

"I'm not sure," said Davy.
Two green ears appeared
over the wall.
They looked up, and saw
the Griffle looking down at them.
"You can come in," said the Griffle.
"Didn't you see the notice?
The Gruffle has gone."

Davy and Hari
went back to the gate.
There was a notice on the gate.
They looked up, and saw the
Griffle.

Hari and Davy went into the garden,
and played hide-and-seek
with the Griffle.
"Remember that **I'm** all green,"
said the Griffle, when at last
they said, "Goodbye".
"Don't go into the garden
if you see two red ears.
Don't go into the garden
if you see a red tail.
Don't go into the garden
if you see a puff of smoke."
"We won't!" said Hari and Davy.
And they went off home,
down the lane.

"Don't go into the garden
if you see two red ears.
Don't go into the garden
if you see a red tail.
Don't go into the garden
if you see a puff of smoke."
"We won't," said Davy
and Hari.

I Spy is a useful reading game.
Use this picture to play it.
"I spy with my little eye
something beginning with..."

(Give the **sound** of the first letter
of the word to be guessed, not the name.)

How can you tell a Griffle from a Gruffle?

How can you tell the **word** Griffle from the **word** Gruffle?
Griffle has an 'if' in the middle.

Gruffle

Griffle

You remember that the Gruffle was very grumpy? 'Gruffle' and 'grumpy' begin with the same sound.
They begin with the same letters.

Peter Puffle and the Gruffle

Puffle and **Gruffle** rhyme.
They both end
in the same sounds.

Look and listen:

Puffle
Gruffle

The words end with
the same letters, too.

Peter
Puffle

Gruffle

Notes for the parent/teacher

Turn back to the beginning, and print the child's name in the space on the title page, using ordinary, not capital letters.

Now go through the book again. Look at each picture and talk about it. Point to the caption below, and read it aloud yourself.

Run your finger along under the words as you read, so that the child learns that reading goes from left to right.

Encourage the child to read the words under the illustrations. Don't rush in with the word before he/she has had time to think, but don't leave him/her struggling too long.

Read this story as often as the child likes hearing it. The more opportunities he/she has of looking at the illustrations and **reading** the captions with you, the more he/she will come to recognise the words.

If you have several books, let the child choose which story he/she would like.

"No, I live in the house at the end of Puddle Lane. But I always come here on Fridays. They have cheese and nuts in the market on Fridays. Come and see."

Jeremy looked down. He looked at one of the tables. There was a big cheese at one end of the table, and a basket of nuts at the other end.

Jeremy looked down.

17